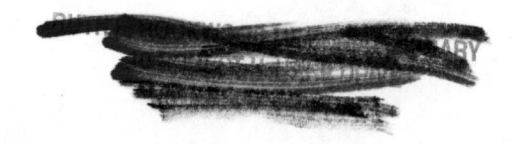

Leo Tolstoy

Published by Peterson Publishing Company, Inc., Mankato, MN.

Designed and Produced by The Creative Spark, San Juan Capistrano, CA.

Copyright ©*2002 by* Peterson Publishing Company, Inc.

Cover photo: Archive Photos

Library of Congress Cataloging-in-Publication Data
Tolstoy, Leo, graf, 1828-1910.
    Leo Tolstoy collected short stories / illustrated by Rob Court.
        p. cm. — (The great author series)
    Includes bibliographical references.
    Contents: Three questions — After the dance — My dream.
    ISBN 0-9709033-0-8
        1. Russia—Juvenile fiction. 2. Children's stories, Russian. [1.
    Russia—Fiction. 2. Short stories.] I. Court, Robert, 1951- ill. II. Title.
    III. Series.

PZ7.T58 Ld 2001
[Fic]—dc21
                                                                    2001021673

LEO TOLSTOY

Collected Short Stories

Illustrated by Rob Court

The Great Author Series

PETERSON PUBLISHING COMPANY, INC.

| THREE QUESTIONS |

I t once occurred to a certain king, that if he always knew the right time to begin everything; if he knew who were the right people to listen to, and whom to avoid, and, above all, if he always knew what was the most important thing to do, he would never fail in anything he might undertake.

And this thought having occurred to him, he had it proclaimed throughout his kingdom that he would give a great reward to anyone who would teach him what was the right time for every action, and who were the most necessary people, and how he might know what was the most important thing to do. And learned men came to the King, but they all answered his questions differently.

In reply to the first question, some said that to know the right time for every action, one must draw up in advance, a table of days, months and years, and must live strictly according to it. Only thus, said they, could everything be done at its proper time. Others declared that it was impossible to decide beforehand the right time for every action; but that, not letting oneself be absorbed in idle pastimes, one should always attend to all that was going on, and then do what was most needful. Others, again, said that however attentive the King might be to what was going on, it was impossible for one man to decide correctly the right time for every action, but that he should have a Council of wise men, who would help him to fix the proper time for everything.

But then again others said there were some things which could not wait to be laid before a Council, but about which one had at once to decide whether to undertake them or not. But in order to decide that one must know beforehand what was going to happen. It is only magicians who know that; and, therefore in order to know the right time for every action, one must consult magicians.

Equally various were the answers to the second question. Some said, the people the King most needed were his councilors; others, the priests; others, the doctors; while some said the warriors were the most necessary.

To the third question, as to what was the most important occupation: some replied that the most important thing in the world was science. Others said it was skill in warfare; and others, again, that it was religious worship.

All the answers being different, the King agreed with none of them, and gave the reward to none. But still wishing to find the right answers to his questions, he decided to consult a hermit, widely renowned for his wisdom.

The hermit lived in a wood which he never quitted and he received none but common folk. So the King put on simple clothes, and before reaching the hermit's cell dismounted from his horse, and, leaving his bodyguard behind, went on alone.

When the King approached, the hermit was digging the ground in front of his hut. Seeing the King, he greeted him and went on digging. The hermit was frail and weak, and each time he stuck his spade into the ground and turned a little earth, he breathed heavily.

The King went up to him and said: "I have come to you, wise hermit, to ask you to answer three questions: How can I learn to do the right thing at the right time? Who are the people I most need, and to whom should I, therefore, pay more attention than to the rest? And, what affairs are the most important and need my first attention?"

The hermit listened to the King, but answered nothing. He just spat on his hand and recommenced digging.

"You are tired," said the King, "let me take the spade and work awhile for you."

"Thanks!" said the hermit, and, giving the spade to the King, he sat down on the ground.

When he had dug two beds, the King stopped and repeated his questions. The hermit again gave no answer, but rose, stretched out his hand for the spade, and said:

"Now rest awhile—and let me work a bit."

But the King did not give him the spade, and continued to dig. One hour passed, and another. The sun began to sink behind the trees, and the King at last stuck the spade into the ground, and said:

"I came to you, wise man, for an answer to my questions. If you can give me none, tell me so, and I will return home."

"Here comes someone running," said the hermit, "let us see who it is."

The King turned round, and saw a bearded man come running out of the woods. The man held his hands pressed against his stomach, and blood was flowing from under them. When he reached the King, he fell fainting on the ground moaning feebly. The King and the hermit unfastened the man's clothing. There was a large wound in his stomach. The King washed it as best he could, and bandaged it with his handkerchief and with a towel the hermit had. But the blood would not stop flowing, and the King again and again removed the bandage soaked with warm blood, and washed and rebandaged the wound. When at last the blood ceased flowing, the man revived and asked for something to drink. The King brought fresh water and gave it to him. Meanwhile the sun had set, and it had become cool. So the King, with the hermit's help, carried the wounded man into the hut and laid him on the bed. Lying on the bed the man closed his eyes and was quiet; but the King was so tired with his walk and with the work he had done, that he crouched down on the threshold, and also fell asleep—so soundly that he slept all through the short summer night. When he awoke in the morning, it was long before he could remember where he was, or who was the strange bearded man lying on the bed and gazing intently at him with shining eyes.

"Forgive me!" said the bearded man in a weak voice, when he saw that the King was awake and was looking at him.

"I do not know you, and have nothing to forgive you for," said the King.

"You do not know me, but I know you. I am that enemy of yours who swore to revenge himself on you, because you executed his brother and seized his property. I knew you had gone alone to see the hermit, and I resolved to kill you on your way back. But the day passed and you did not return. So I came out from my ambush to find you, and I came upon your body-guard, and they recognized me, and wounded me. I escaped from them, but should have bled to death had you not dressed my wound. I wished to kill you, and you have saved my life. Now, if I live, and if you wish it, I will serve you as your most faithful slave, and will bid my sons do the same. Forgive me!"

The King was very glad to have made peace with his enemy so easily, and to have gained him for a friend, and he not only forgave him, but said he would send his servants and his own physician to attend him, and promised to restore his property.

Having taken leave of the wounded man, the King went out into the porch and looked around for the hermit. Before going away he wished once more to beg an answer to the

questions he had put. The hermit was outside, on his knees, sowing seeds in the beds that had been dug the day before.

The King approached him, and said:

"For the last time, I pray you to answer my questions, wise man."

"You have already been answered!" said the hermit still crouching on his thin legs, and looking up at the King, who stood before him.

"How answered? What do you mean?" asked the King.

"Do you not see," replied the hermit. "If you had not pitied my weakness yesterday, and had not dug these beds for me, but had gone your way, that man would have attacked you, and you would have repented of not having stayed with me. So the most important time was when you were digging the beds; and I was the most important man; and to do me good was your most important business. Afterwards, when that man ran to us, the most important time was when you were attending to him, for if you had not bound up his wounds he would have died without having made peace with you. So he was the most important man, and what you did for him was your most important business.

"Remember then: there is only one time that is important—Now! It is the most important time because it is the only time when we have any power. The most necessary man is he with whom you are, for no man knows whether he will ever have dealings with anyone else; and the most important affair is to do him good, because for that purpose alone was man sent into this life!"

| AFTER THE DANCE |

"And you say that a man cannot, of himself, understand what is good and evil; that it is all environment, that the environment swamps the man. But I believe it is all chance. Take my own case ..."

Thus spoke our excellent friend, Ivan Vasilievich, after a conversation between us on the impossibility of improving individual character without a change of the conditions under which men live. Nobody had actually said that one could not of oneself understand good and evil; but it was a habit of Ivan Vasilievich to answer in this way the thoughts aroused in his own mind by conversation, and to illustrate those thoughts by relating incidents in his own life. He often quite forgot the reason for his story in telling it; but he always told it with great sincerity and feeling.

He did so now.

"Take my own case. My whole life was molded, not by environment, but by something quite different."

"By what, then?" we asked.

"Oh, that is a long story. I should have to tell you about a great many things to make you understand."

"Well, tell us then."

Ivan Vasilievich thought a little, and shook his head.

"My whole life," he said, "was changed in one night, or, rather, morning."

"Why, what happened?" one of us asked.

"What happened was that I was very much in love. I have been in love many times, but this was the most serious of all. It is a thing of the past; she has married daughters now. It was Varinka B—— "

Ivan Vasilievich mentioned her surname. "Even at fifty, she is remarkably handsome; but in her youth, at eighteen, she was exquisite—tall, slender, graceful, and stately. Yes, stately is the word; she held herself very erect, by instinct as it were; and carried her head high, and that together with her beauty and height gave her a queenly air in spite of being thin, even bony one might say. It might indeed have been deterring had it not been for her smile, which was always gay and cordial, and for the charming light in her eyes and for her youthful sweetness."

"What an entrancing description you give, Ivan Vasilievich!"

"Description, indeed! I could not possibly describe her so that you could appreciate her. But that does not matter; what I am going to tell you happened in the forties. I was at that time a student in a provincial university. I don't know whether it was a good thing or no, but we had no political clubs, no theories in our universities then. We were simply young and spent our time as young men do, studying and amusing ourselves. I was a very gay, lively, careless fellow, and had plenty of money too. I had a fine horse, and used to go tobogganing with the young ladies. Skating had not yet come into fashion. I went to drinking parties with my comrades—in those days we drank nothing but champagne—if we had no champagne we drank nothing at all. We never drank vodka, as they do now. Evening parties and balls were my favorite amusements. I danced well, and was not an ugly fellow."

"Come, there is no need to be modest," interrupted a lady near him. "We have seen your photograph. Not ugly, indeed! You were a handsome fellow."

"Handsome, if you like. That does not matter. When my love for her was at its strongest, on the last day of the carnival, I was at a ball at the provincial marshall's, a good-natured old man, rich and hospitable, and a court chamberlain. The guests were welcomed by his wife, who was as good-natured as himself. She was dressed in puce-colored velvet, and had a diamond diadem on her forehead, and her plump, old white shoulders and bosom were bare like the portraits of Empress Elizabeth, the daughter of Peter the Great.

"It was a delightful ball. It was a splendid room, with a gallery for the orchestra, which was famous at the time, and consisted of serfs belonging to a musical landowner. The refreshments were magnificent, and the champagne flowed in rivers. Though I was fond of champagne I did not drink that night, because without it I was drunk with love. But I made up for it by dancing waltzes and polkas till I was ready to drop—of course, whenever possible, with Varinka. She wore a white dress with a pink sash, white shoes, and white kid gloves, which did not quite reach to her thin pointed elbows. A disgusting engineer named Anisimov robbed me of the mazurka with her—to this day I cannot forgive him. He asked her for the dance the minute she arrived, while I had driven to the hair-dresser's to get a pair of gloves, and was late. So I did not dance the mazurka with her, but with a German girl to whom I had previously paid a little attention; but I am afraid I did not behave very politely to her that evening. I hardly spoke or looked at her, and saw nothing but the tall, slender figure in a white dress, with a pink sash, a flushed, beaming, dimpled face, and sweet, kind eyes. I was not alone; they were all looking at her with admiration, the men and women alike, although she outshone all of them. They could not help admiring her.

"Although I was not nominally her partner for the mazurka, I did as a matter of fact dance nearly the whole time with her. She always came forward boldly the whole length of the room to pick me out. I flew to meet her without waiting to be chosen, and she thanked me with a smile for my intuition. When I was brought up to her with somebody else, and she guessed wrongly, she took the other man's hand with a shrug of her slim shoulders, and smiled at me regretfully.

"Whenever there was a waltz figure in the mazurka, I waltzed with her for a long time, and breathing fast and smiling, she would say, 'Encore'; and I went on waltzing and waltzing, as though unconscious of any bodily existence."

"Come now, how could you be unconscious of it with your arm round her waist? You must have been conscious, not only of your own existence, but of hers," said one of the party.

Ivan Vasilievich cried out, almost shouting in anger: "There you are, moderns all over! Nowadays you think of nothing but the body. It was different in our day. The more I was in love the less corporeal was she in my eyes. Nowadays you see legs, ankles, and I don't know what. You undress the women you are in love with. In my eyes, as Alphonse Karr said—and he was a good writer—'the one I loved was always draped in robes of bronze.' We never thought of doing so; we tried to veil her nakedness, like Noah's good-natured son. Oh, well, you can't understand."

"Don't pay any attention to him. Go on," said one of them.

"Well, I danced for the most part with her, and did not notice how time was passing. The musicians kept playing the same mazurka tunes over and over again in desperate exhaustion—you know what it is toward the end of a ball. Papas and mammas were already getting up from the card-tables in the drawing-room in expectation of supper, the men-servants were running to and fro bringing in things. It was nearly three o'clock. I had to make the most of the last minutes. I chose her again for the mazurka, and for the hundredth time we danced across the room.

" 'The quadrille after supper is mine,' I said, taking her to her place.

" 'Of course, if I am not carried off home,' she said, with a smile.

" 'I won't give you up,' I said.

" 'Give me my fan, anyhow,' she answered.

" 'I am so sorry to part with it,' I said, handing her a cheap white fan.

" 'Well, here's something to console you,' she said, plucking a feather out of the fan, and giving it to me.

"I took the feather, and could only express my rapture and gratitude with my eyes. I was not only pleased and gay, I was happy, delighted; I was good, I was not myself but some being not of this earth, knowing nothing of evil. I hid the feather in my glove, and stood there unable to tear myself away from her.

" 'Look, they are urging father to dance,' she said to me, pointing to the tall, stately figure of her father, a colonel with silver epaulettes, who was standing in the doorway with some ladies.

" 'Varinka, come here!' exclaimed our hostess, the lady with the diamond ferronniere and with shoulders like Elizabeth, in a loud voice.

" 'Varinka went to the door, and I followed her.

" 'Persuade your father to dance the mazurka with you, ma chere.—Do, please, Peter Valdislavovich,' she said, turning to the colonel.

"Varinka's father was a very handsome, well-preserved old man. He had a good color, moustaches curled in the style of Nicolas I, and white whiskers which met the moustaches. His hair was combed on to his forehead, and a bright smile, like his daughter's, was on his lips and in his eyes. He was splendidly set up, with a broad military chest, on which he wore some decorations, and he had powerful shoulders and long slim legs. He was that ultra-military type produced by the discipline of Emperor Nicolas I.

"When we approached the door the colonel was just refusing to dance, saying that he had quite forgotten how; but at that instant he smiled, swung his arm gracefully around to the left, drew his sword from its sheath, handed it to an obliging young man who stood near, and smoothed his suede glove on his right hand.

" 'Everything must be done according to rule,' he said with a smile. He took the hand of his daughter, and stood one-quarter turned, waiting for the music.

"At the first sound of the mazurka, he stamped one foot smartly, threw the other forward, and, at first slowly and smoothly, then buoyantly and impetuously, with stamping of feet and clicking of boots, his tall, imposing figure moved the length of the room. Varinka swayed gracefully beside him, rhythmically and easily, making her steps short or long, with her little feet in their white satin slippers.

"All the people in the room followed every movement of the couple. As for me I not only admired, I regarded them with enraptured sympathy. I was particularly impressed with the old gentleman's boots. They were not the modern pointed affairs, but were made of cheap leather, squared-toed, and evidently

built by the regimental cobbler. In order that his daughter might dress and go out in society, he did not buy fashionable boots, but wore homemade ones, I thought, and his square toes seemed to me most touching. It was obvious that in his time he had been a good dancer; but now he was too heavy, and his legs had not spring enough for all the beautiful steps he tried to take. Still, he contrived to go twice round the room. When at the end, standing with legs apart, he suddenly clicked his feet together and fell on one knee, a bit heavily, and she danced gracefully around him, smiling and adjusting her skirt, the whole room applauded.

"Rising with an effort, he tenderly took his daughter's face between his hands. He kissed her on the forehead, and brought her to me, under the impression that I was her partner for the mazurka. I said I was not. 'Well, never mind. Just go around the room once with her,' he said, smiling kindly, as he replaced his sword in the sheath.

"As the contents of a bottle flow readily when the first drop has been poured, so my love for Varinka seemed to set free the whole force of loving within me. In surrounding her it embraced the world. I loved the hostess with her diadem and her shoulders like Elizabeth, and her husband and her guests and her footmen, and even the engineer Anisimov who felt peevish toward me. As for Varinka's father, with his homemade boots and his kind smile, so like her own, I felt a sort of tenderness for him that was almost rapture.

"After supper I danced the promised quadrille with her, and though I had been infinitely happy before, I grew still happier every moment.

"We did not speak of love. I neither asked myself nor her whether she loved me. It was quite enough to know that I loved her. And I had only one fear—that something might come to interfere with my great joy.

"When I went home, and began to undress for the night, I found it quite out of the question. I held the little feather out of her fan in my hand, and one of her gloves which she gave me when I helped her into the carriage after her mother. Looking at these things, and without closing my eyes, I could see her before me as she was for an instant when she had to choose between two partners. She tried to guess what kind of person was represented in me, and I could hear her sweet voice as she said, 'Pride—am I right?' and merrily gave me her hand. At supper she took the first sip from my glass of champagne, looking at me over the rim with her caressing glance. But, plainest of all, I could see her as she danced with her father, gliding along beside him, and looking at the admiring observers with pride and happiness.

"He and she were united in my mind in one rush of pathetic tenderness.

"I was living then with my brother, who has since died. He disliked going out, and never went to dances; and besides, he was busy preparing for his last university examinations, and was leading a very regular life. He was asleep. I looked at him, his head buried in the pillow and half covered with the quilt;

and I affectionately pitied him, pitied him for his ignorance of the bliss I was experiencing. Our serf Petrusha had met me with a candle, ready to undress me, but I sent him away. His sleepy face and tousled hair seemed to me so touching. Trying not to make a noise, I went to my room on tiptoe and sat down on my bed. No, I was too happy; I could not sleep. Besides, it was too hot in the rooms. Without taking off my uniform, I went quietly into the hall, put on my overcoat, opened the front door and stepped out into the street.

"It was after four when I had left the ball; going home and stopping there a while had occupied two hours, so by the time I went out it was dawn. It was regular carnival weather— foggy, and the road full of water-soaked snow just melting, and water dripping from the eaves. Varinka's family lived on the edge of town near a large field, one end of which was a parade ground: at the other end was a boarding-school for young ladies. I passed through our empty little street and came to the main thoroughfare, where I met pedestrians and sledges laden with wood, the runners grating the road. The horses swung with regular paces beneath their shining yokes, their backs covered with straw mats and their heads wet with rain; while the drivers, in enormous boots, splashed through the mud beside the sledges. All this, the very horses themselves, seemed to me stimulating and fascinating, full of suggestion.

"When I approached the field near their house, I saw at one end of it, in the direction of the parade ground, some-thing very huge and black, and I heard sounds of fife and drum proceeding from it. My heart had been full of song, and

I had heard in imagination the tune of the mazurka, but this was very harsh music. It was not pleasant.

" 'What can that be?' I thought, and went toward the sound by a slippery path through the center of the field. Walking about a hundred paces, I began to distinguish many black objects through the mist. They were evidently soldiers. 'It is probably a drill,' I thought.

"So I went along in that direction in company with a blacksmith, who wore a dirty coat and an apron, and was carrying something. He walked ahead of me as we approached the place. The soldiers in black uniforms stood in two rows, facing each other motionless, their guns at rest. Behind them stood the fifes and drums, incessantly repeating the same unpleasant tune.

" 'What are they doing?' I asked the blacksmith, who halted at my side.

" 'A Tartar is being beaten through the ranks for his attempt to desert,' said the blacksmith in an angry tone, as he looked intently at the far end of the line.

"I looked in the same direction, and saw between the files something horrid approaching me. The thing that approached was a man, stripped to the waist, fastened with cords to the guns of two soldiers who were leading him. At his side an officer in overcoat and cap was walking, whose figure had a familiar look. The victim advanced under the blows that rained upon him from both sides, his whole body plunging, his feet dragging through the snow. Now he threw himself backward, and the subalterns who led him thrust him forward. Now he fell forward, and they pulled him up short; while ever at his side marched the tall officer, with firm and nervous pace. It was Varinka's father, with his rosy face and white moustache.

"At each stroke the man, as if amazed, turned his face, grimacing with pain, toward the side whence the blow came, and showing his white teeth repeated the same words over and over. But I could only hear what the words were when he came quite near. He did not speak them, he sobbed them out,—" 'Brothers, have mercy on me! Brothers, have mercy on me!' But the brothers had, no mercy, and when the procession came close to me, I saw how a soldier who stood opposite me took a firm step forward and lifting his stick with a whirr, brought it down upon the man's back. The man plunged forward, but the subalterns pulled him back, and another blow came down from the other side, then from this side and then from the other. The colonel marched beside him, and looking now at his feet and now at the man, inhaled the air, puffed out his cheeks, and breathed it out between his protruded lips.

When they passed the place where I stood, I caught a glimpse between the two files of the back of the man that was being punished. It was something so many-colored, wet, red, unnatural, that I could hardly believe it was a human body.

" 'My God!' muttered the blacksmith.

The procession moved farther away. The blows continued to rain upon the writhing, falling creature; the fifes shrilled and the drums beat, and the tall imposing figure of the colonel moved alongside the man, just as before. Then, suddenly, the colonel stopped, and rapidly approached a man in the ranks.

" 'I'll teach you to hit him gently,' I heard his furious voice say. 'Will you pat him like that? Will you?' and I saw how his strong hand in the suede glove struck the weak, bloodless, terrified soldier for not bringing down his stick with sufficient strength on the red neck of the Tartar.

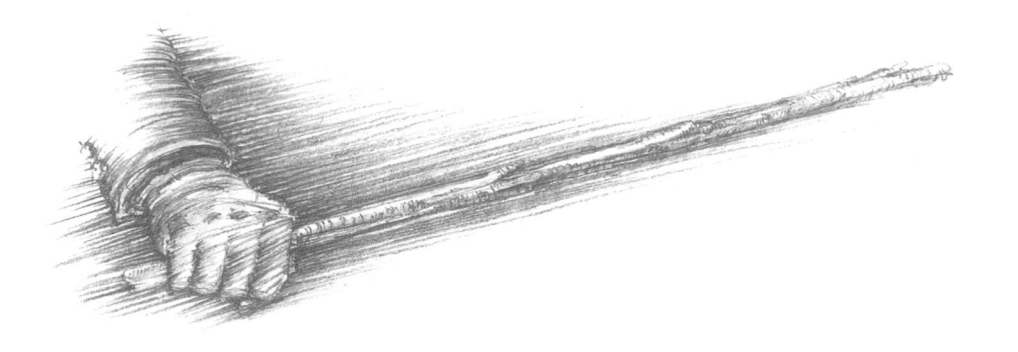

" 'Bring new sticks!' he cried, and looking round, he saw me. Assuming an air of not knowing me, and with a ferocious, angry frown, he hastily turned away. I felt so utterly ashamed that I didn't know where to look. It was as if I had been detected in a disgraceful act. I dropped my eyes, and quickly hurried home. All the way I had the drums beating and the fifes whistling in my ears. And I heard the words, 'Brothers, have mercy on me!' or 'Will you pat him? Will you?' My heart was full of physical disgust that was almost sickness. So much so that I halted several times on my way, for I had the feeling that I was going to be really sick from all the horrors that possessed me at that sight. I do not remember how I got home and got to bed. But the moment I was about to fall asleep I heard and saw again all that had happened, and I sprang up.

" 'Evidently he knows something I do not know,' I thought about the colonel. "If I knew what he knows I should certainly grasp—understand—what I have just seen, and it would not cause me such suffering.'

"But however much I thought about it, I could not understand the thing that the colonel knew. It was evening before I could get to sleep, and then only after calling on a friend and drinking till I; was quite drunk.

"Do you think I had come to the conclusion that the deed I had witnessed was wicked? Oh, no. Since it was done with such assurance, and was recognized by everyone as indispensable, they doubtless knew something which I did not know. So I thought, and tried to understand. But no matter, I could never understand it, then or afterwards. And not being able to grasp it, I could not enter the service as I had intended. I don't mean only the military service: I did not enter the Civil Service either. And so I have been of no use whatever, as you can see."

"Yes, we know how useless you've been," said one of us. "Tell us, rather, how many people would be of any use at all if it hadn't been for you."

"Oh, that's utter nonsense," said Ivan Vasilievich, with genuine annoyance.

"Well; and what about the love affair?

"My love? It decreased from that day. When, as often happened, she looked dreamy and meditative, I instantly recollected the colonel on the parade ground, and I felt so awkward and uncomfortable that I began to see her less frequently. So my love came to naught. Yes; such chances arise, and they alter and direct a man's whole life," he said in summing up. "And you say …"

| My Dream |

"As a daughter she no longer exists for me. Can't you understand? She simply doesn't exist. Still, I cannot possibly leave her to the charity of strangers. I will arrange things so that she can live as she pleases, but I do not wish to hear of her. Who would ever have thought … the horror of it, the horror of it."

He shrugged his shoulders, shook his head, and raised his eyes. These words were spoken by Prince Michael Ivanovich to his brother Peter, who was governor of a province in Central Russia. Prince Peter was a man of fifty, Michael's junior by ten years.

On discovering that his daughter, who had left his house a year before, had settled here with her child, the elder brother had come from St. Petersburg to the provincial town, where the above conversation took place.

Prince Michael Ivanovich was a tall, handsome, white-haired, fresh colored man, proud and attractive in appearance and bearing. His family consisted of a vulgar, irritable wife, who wrangled with him continually over every petty detail, a son, a ne'er-do-well, spendthrift and roue—yet a "gentleman," according to his father's code, two daughters, of whom the elder had married well, and was living in St. Petersburg; and the younger, Lisa—his favorite, who had disappeared from home a year before. Only a short while ago, he had found her with her child in this provincial town.

Prince Peter wanted to ask his brother how, and under what circumstances, Lisa had left home, and who could possibly be the father of her child. But he could not make up his mind to inquire. That very morning, when his wife had attempted to condole with her brother-in-law, Prince Peter had observed a look of pain on his brother's face. The look had at once been masked by an expression of unapproachable pride, and he had begun to question her about their flat and the price she paid. At luncheon, before the family and guests, he had been witty and sarcastic as usual. Toward everyone, except the children, whom he treated with almost reverent tenderness, he adopted an attitude of distant hauteur. And yet it was so natural to him that everyone somehow acknowledged his right to be haughty.

In the evening, his brother arranged a game of whist. When he retired to the room that had been made ready for him and was just beginning to take out his artificial teeth, some one tapped lightly on the door with two fingers.

"Who is that?"

"*C'est moi*, Michael."

Prince Michael Ivanovich recognized the voice of his sister-in-law, frowned, replaced his teeth, and said to himself, "What does she want?" Aloud he said, "*Entrez*."

His sister-in-law was a quiet, gentle creature, who bowed in submission to her husband's will. But to many, she seemed a crank, and some did not hesitate to call her a fool. She was pretty, but her hair was always carelessly dressed, and she herself was untidy and absent-minded. She had, also, the strangest, most unaristocratic ideas, by no means fitting in the wife of a high official. These ideas she would express most unexpectedly, to everybody's astonishment, her husband's no less than her friends'.

"*Fous pouvez me renvoyer, mais je ne m'en irai pas, je vous le dis d'avance*," she began, in her characteristic, indifferent way.

"*Dieu preserve*," answered her brother-in-law, with his usual somewhat exaggerated politeness, and brought forward a chair for her.

"*Ca ne vous derange pas?*" she asked, taking out a cigarette. "I'm not going to say anything unpleasant, Michael. I only wanted to say something about Lisochka."

Michael Ivanovich sighed—the word pained him; but mastering himself at once, he answered with a tired smile.

"Our conversation can only be on one subject, and that is the subject you wish to discuss " He spoke without looking at her, and avoided even naming the subject. But his plump, pretty little sister-in-law was unabashed. She continued to regard him with the same gentle, imploring look in her blue eyes, sighing even more deeply.

"Michael, *mon bon ami,* have pity on her. She is only human."

"I never doubted that," said Michael Ivanovich with a bitter smile.

"She is your daughter."

"She was—but my dear Aline, why talk about this?"

"Michael, dear, won't you see her? I only wanted to say, that the one who is to blame—"

Prince Michael Ivanovich flushed; his face became cruel.

"For heaven's sake, let us stop. I have suffered enough. I have now but one desire, and that is to put her in such a position that she will be independent of others, and that she shall have no further need of communicating with me. Then she can live her own life, and my family and I need know nothing more about her. That is all I can do."

"Michael, you say nothing but 'I'! She, too, is 'I.' "

"No doubt; but, dear Aline, please let us drop the matter. I feel it too deeply."

Alexandra Dmitrievna remained silent for a few moments, shaking her head. "And Masha, your wife, thinks as you do?"

"Yes, quite."

Alexandra Dmitrievna made an inarticulate sound.

"Brisons la dessus et bonne nuit," said he. But she did not go. She stood silent a moment. Then, "Peter tells me you intend to leave the money with the woman where she lives. Have you the address?"

"I have."

"Don't leave it with the woman, Michael! Go yourself. Just see how she lives. If you don't want to see her, you need not. HE isn't there; there is no one there."

Michael Ivanovich shuddered violently.

"Why do you torture me so? It's a sin against hospitality!"

Alexandra Dmitrievna rose, and almost in tears, being touched by her own pleading, said, "She is so miserable, but she is such a dear."

He got up, and stood waiting for her to finish. She held out her hand.

"Michael, you do wrong," said she, and left him.

For a long while after she had gone Michael Ivanovich walked to and fro on the square of carpet. He frowned and

shivered, and exclaimed, "Oh, oh!" And then the sound of his own voice frightened him, and he was silent.

His wounded pride tortured him. His daughter—his—brought up in the house of her mother, the famous Avdotia Borisovna, whom the Empress honored with her visits, and acquaintance with whom was an honor for all the world! His daughter—and he had lived his life as a knight of old, knowing neither fear nor blame. The fact that he had a natural son born of a Frenchwoman, whom he had settled abroad, did not lower his own self-esteem. And now this daughter, for whom he had not only done everything that a father could and should do; this daughter to whom he had given a splendid education and every opportunity to make a match in the best Russian society—this daughter to whom he had not only given all that a girl could desire, but whom he had really *loved;* whom he had admired, been proud of—this daughter had repaid him with such disgrace, that he was ashamed and could not face the eyes of men!

He recalled the time when she was not merely his child, and a member of his family, but his darling, his joy and his pride. He saw her again, a little thing of eight or nine, bright, intelligent, lively, impetuous, graceful, with brilliant black eyes and flowing auburn hair. He remembered how she used to jump up on his knees and hug him, and tickle his neck; and how she would laugh, regardless of his protests, and continue to tickle him, and kiss his lips, his eyes, and his cheeks. He was naturally opposed to all demonstration, but this impetuous love moved him, and he often submitted to her petting. He remembered also how sweet it was to caress her. To remember all this, when that sweet child had become what she now was, a creature of whom he could not think without loathing.

He also recalled the time when she was growing into womanhood, and the curious feeling of fear and anger that he experienced when he became aware that men regarded her as a woman. He thought of his jealous love when she came coquettishly to him dressed for a ball, and knowing that she was pretty. He dreaded the passionate glances which fell upon her, that she not only did not understand but rejoiced in. "Yes," thought he, "that superstition of woman's purity! Quite the contrary, they do not know shame—they lack this sense " He remembered how, quite inexplicably to him, she had refused two very good suitors. She had become more and more fascinated by her own success in the round of gaieties she lived in.

But this success could not last long. A year passed, then two, then three. She was a familiar figure, beautiful—but her first youth had passed, and she had become somehow part of the ballroom furniture. Michael Ivanovich remembered how he had realized that she was on the road to spinsterhood and desired but one thing for her. He must get her married off as quickly as possible, perhaps not quite so well as might have been arranged earlier, but still a respectable match.

But it seemed to him she had behaved with a pride that bordered on insolence. Remembering this, his anger rose more and more fiercely against her. To think of her refusing so many decent men, only to end in this disgrace. "Oh, oh!" he groaned again.

Then stopping, he lit a cigarette, and tried to think of other things. He would send her money, without ever letting her see him. But memories came again. He remembered—it was not so very long ago, for she was more than twenty then—her beginning a flirtation with a boy of fourteen, a cadet of the Corps of Pages who had been staying with them in the country. She had driven the boy half crazy; he had wept in his distraction. Then how she had rebuked her father severely, coldly, and even rudely, when, to put an end to this stupid affair, he had sent the boy away. She seemed somehow to consider herself insulted. Since then father and daughter had drifted into undisguised hostility.

"I was right," he said to himself. "She is a wicked and shameless woman."

And then, as a last ghastly memory, there was the letter from Moscow, in which she wrote that she could not return home; that she was a miserable, abandoned woman, asking only to be forgiven and forgotten. Then the horrid recollection of the scene with his wife came to him; their surmises and their suspicions, which became a certainty. The calamity had happened in Finland, where they had let her visit her aunt; and the culprit was an insignificant Swede, a student, an empty-headed, worthless creature—and married.

All this came back to him now as he paced backwards and forwards on the bedroom carpet, recollecting his former love for her, his pride in her. He recoiled with terror before the incomprehensible fact of her downfall, and he hated her for the agony she was causing him. He remembered the conversation with his sister-in-law and tried to imagine how he might forgive her. But as soon as the thought of "him" arose, there surged up in his heart horror, disgust, and wounded pride. He groaned aloud and tried to think of something else.

"No, it is impossible; I will hand over the money to Peter to give her monthly. And as for me, I have no longer a daughter."

And again a curious feeling overpowered him: a mixture of self-pity at the recollection of his love for her, and of fury against her for causing him this anguish.

II

During the last year Lisa had without doubt lived through more than in all the preceding twenty-five. Suddenly she had realized the emptiness of her whole life. It rose before her, base and sordid—this life at home and among the rich set in St. Petersburg—this animal existence that never sounded the depths, but only touched the shallows of life.

It was well enough for a year or two, or perhaps even three. But when it went on for seven or eight years, with its parties, balls, concerts, and suppers; with its costumes and coiffures to display the charms of the body; with its adorers old and young, all alike seemingly possessed of some unaccountable right to have everything, to laugh at everything; and with its summer months spent in the same way, everything yielding but a superficial pleasure, even music and reading merely touching upon life's problems, but never solving them—all this holding out no promise of change, and losing its charm more and more—she began to despair. She had desperate moods when she longed to die.

Her friends directed her thoughts to charity. On the one hand, she saw poverty which was real and repulsive, and a sham poverty even more repulsive and pitiable; on the other, she saw the terrible indifference of the lady patronesses who came in carriages and gowns worth thousands. Life became to her more and more unbearable. She yearned for something real, for life itself—not this playing at living, not this skimming life of its cream. Of real life there was none. The best of her memories was her love for the little cadet Koko. That had been a good, honest, straightforward impulse, and now there was nothing like it. There could not be. She grew more and more depressed, and in this gloomy mood she went to visit an aunt in Finland. The fresh scenery and surroundings, the people strangely different to her own, appealed to her at any rate as a new experience.

How and when it all began she could not clearly remember. Her aunt had another guest, a Swede. He talked of his work, his people, the latest Swedish novel. Somehow, she herself did not know how that terrible fascination of glances and smiles began, the meaning of which cannot be put into words.

These smiles and glances seemed to reveal to each, not only the soul of the other, but some vital and universal mystery. Every word they spoke was invested by these smiles with a profound and wonderful significance. Music, too, when they were listening together, or when they sang duets, became full of the same deep meaning. So, also, the words in the books they read aloud. Sometimes they would argue, but the moment their eyes met, or a smile flashed between them, the discussion remained far behind. They soared beyond it to some higher plane consecrated to themselves.

How it had come about, how and when the devil, who had seized hold of them both, first appeared behind these smiles and glances, she could not say. But, when terror first seized her, the invisible threads that bound them were already so

interwoven that she had no power to tear herself free. She could only count on him and on his honor. She hoped that he would not make use of his power; yet all the while she vaguely desired it.

Her weakness was the greater, because she had nothing to support her in the struggle. She was weary of society life and she had no affection for her mother. Her father, so she thought, had cast her away from him, and she longed passionately to live and to have done with play. Love, the perfect love of a woman for a man, held the promise of life for her. Her strong, passionate nature, too, was dragging her thither. In the tall, strong figure of this man, with his fair hair and light upturned moustache, under which shone a smile attractive and compelling, she saw the promise of that life for which she longed. And then the smiles and glances, the hope of something so incredibly beautiful, led, as they were bound to lead, to that which she feared but unconsciously awaited. Suddenly all that was beautiful, joyous, spiritual, and full of promise for the future, became animal and sordid, sad and despairing.

She looked into his eyes and tried to smile, pretending that she feared nothing, that everything was as it should be; but deep down in her soul she knew it was all over. She understood that she had not found in him what she had sought; that which she had once known in herself and in Koko. She told him that he must write to her father asking her hand in marriage. This he promised to do; but when she met him next he said it was impossible for him to write just then. She saw something vague and furtive in his eyes, and her distrust of him grew. The following day he wrote to her, telling her that he was already married, though his wife had left him long since; that he knew she would despise him for the wrong he had done her, and implored her forgiveness. She made him come to see her. She said she loved him; that she felt herself bound to him forever whether he was married or not, and would never leave him. The next time they met he told her that he and his parents were so poor that he could only offer her the meanest existence. She answered that she needed nothing, and was ready to go with him at once wherever he wished. He endeavoured to dissuade her, advising her to wait; and so she waited. But to live on with this secret, with occasional meetings, and merely corresponding with him, all hidden from her family, was agonising, and she insisted again that he must take her away. At first, when she returned to St. Petersburg, he wrote promising to come, and then letters ceased and she knew no more of him.

She tried to lead her old life, but it was impossible. She fell ill, and the efforts of the doctors were unavailing; in her hopelessness she resolved to kill herself. But how was she to do this, so that her death might seem natural? She really desired to take her life, and imagined that she had irrevocably decided on the step. So, obtaining some poison, she poured it into a glass, and in another instant would have drunk it, had not her sister's little son of five at that very moment run in to show her a toy his grandmother had given him. She caressed the child, and, suddenly stopping short, burst into tears.

The thought overpowered her that she, too, might have been a mother had he not been married, and this vision of motherhood made her look into her own soul for the first time. She began to think not of what others would say of her, but of her own life. To kill oneself because of what the world might say was easy; but the moment she saw her own life dissociated from the world, to take that life was out of the question. She threw away the poison, and ceased to think of suicide.

Then her life within began. It was real life, and despite the torture of it, had the possibility been given her, she would not have turned back from it. She began to pray, but there was no comfort in prayer; and her suffering was less for herself than for her father, whose grief she foresaw and understood.

Thus months dragged along, and then something happened which entirely transformed her life. One day, when she was at work upon a quilt, she suddenly experienced a strange sensation. No—it seemed impossible. Motionless she sat with her work in hand. Was it possible that this was *it*. Forgetting everything, his baseness and deceit, her mother's querulousness, and her father's sorrow, she smiled. She shuddered at the recollection that she was on the point of killing it, together with herself.

She now directed all her thoughts to getting away—somewhere where she could bear her child—and become a miserable, pitiful mother, but a mother withal. Somehow she planned and arranged it all, leaving her home and settling in a distant provincial town, where no one could find her, and where she thought she would be far from her people. But, unfortunately, her father's brother received an appointment there, a thing she could not possibly foresee. For four months she had been living in the house of a midwife—one Maria Ivanovna; and, on learning that her uncle had come to the town, she was preparing to fly to a still remoter hiding place.

III

MICHAEL IVANOVICH awoke early next morning. He entered his brother's study, and handed him the check, filled in for a sum which he asked him to pay in monthly installments to his daughter. He inquired when the express left for St. Petersburg. The train left at seven in the evening, giving him time for an early dinner before leaving. He breakfasted with his sister-in-law, who refrained from mentioning the subject which was so painful to him, but only looked at him timidly; and after breakfast he went out for his regular morning walk.

Alexandra Dmitrievna followed him into the hall.

"Go into the public gardens, Michael—it is very charming there, and quite near to everything," said she, meeting his somber looks with a pathetic glance.

Michael Ivanovich followed her advice and went to the public gardens, which were so near to everything, and meditated with annoyance on the stupidity, the obstinacy, and heartlessness of women.

"She is not in the very least sorry for me," he thought of his sister-in-law. "She cannot even understand my sorrow. And what of her?" He was thinking of his daughter. "She knows what all this means to me—the torture. What a blow in one's old age! My days will be shortened by it! But I'd rather have it over than endure this agony. And all that *'pour les beaux yeux d'un chenapan'*—oh!" he moaned; and a wave of hatred and fury arose in him as he thought of what would be said in the town when everyone knew. (And no doubt everyone knew already.) Such a feeling of rage possessed him that he would have liked to beat it into her head, and make her understand what she had done. These women never understand. "It is quite near every-thing," suddenly came to his mind, and getting out his notebook, he found her address. Vera Ivanovna Silvestrova, Kukonskaya Street, Abromov's house. She was living under this name. He left the gardens and called a cab.

"Whom do you wish to see, sir?" asked the midwife, Maria Ivanovna, when he stepped on the narrow landing of the steep, stuffy staircase.

"Does Madame Silvestrova live here?"

"Vera Ivanovna? Yes; please come in. She has gone out; she's gone to the shop round the corner. But she'll be back in a minute."

Michael Ivanovich followed the stout figure of Maria Ivanovna into a tiny parlour, and from the next room came the screams of a baby, sounding cross and peevish, which filled him with disgust. They cut him like a knife.

Maria Ivanovna apologized, and went into the room, and he could hear her soothing the child. The child became quiet, and she returned.

"That is her baby; she'll be back in a minute. You are a friend of hers, I suppose?"

"Yes—a friend—but I think I had better come back later on," said Michael Ivanovich, preparing to go. It was too unbearable, this preparation to meet her, and any explanation seemed impossible.

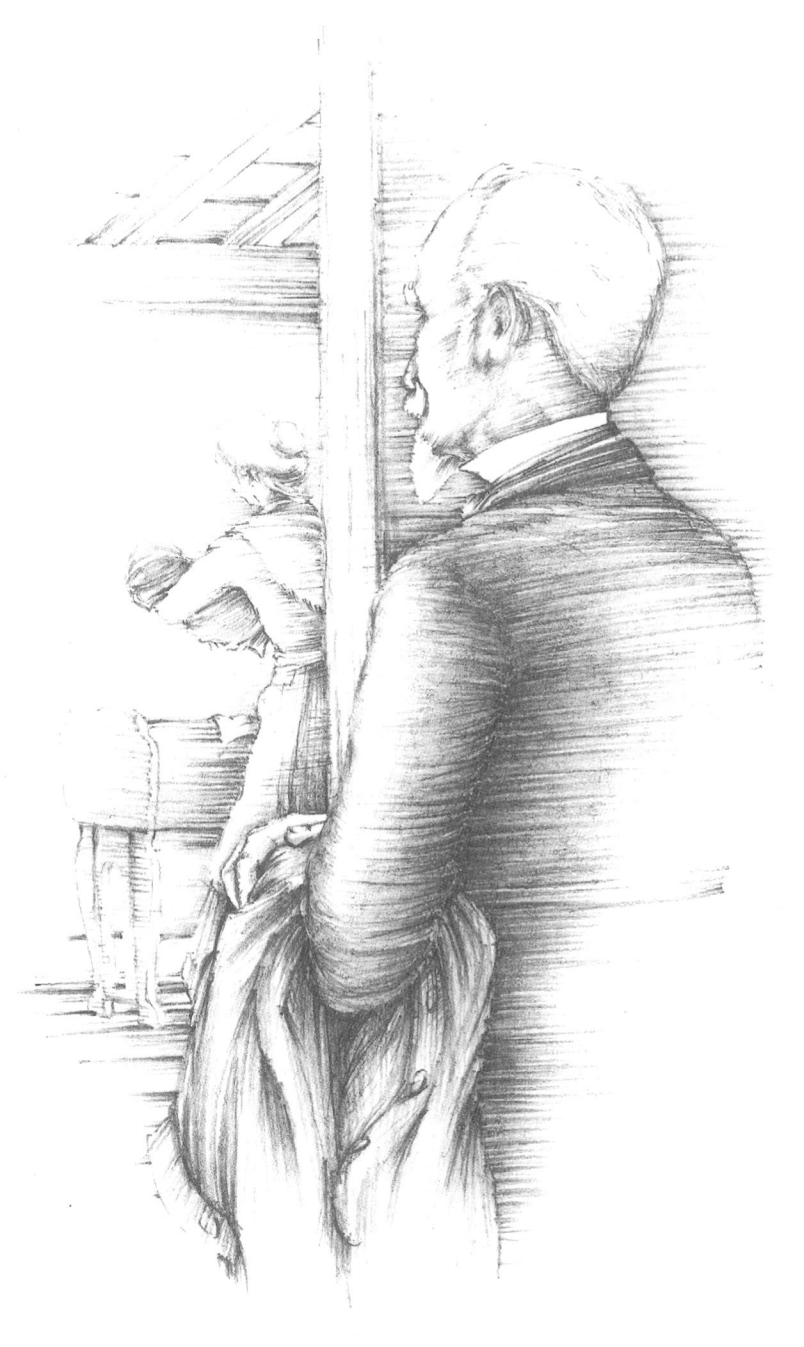

He had just turned to leave, when he heard quick, light steps on the stairs, and he recognized Lisa's voice.

"Maria Ivanovna—has he been crying while I've been gone—I was—"

Then she saw her father. The parcel she was carrying fell from her hands.

"Father!" she cried, and stopped in the doorway, white and trembling. He remained motionless, staring at her. She had grown so thin. Her eyes were larger, her nose sharper, her hands worn and bony. He neither knew what to do, nor what to say. He forgot all his grief about his dishonor. He only felt sorrow, infinite sorrow for her; sorrow for her thinness, and for her miserable rough clothing; and most of all, for her pitiful face and imploring eyes.

"Father—forgive," she said, moving toward him.

"Forgive—forgive me," he murmured; and he began to sob like a child, kissing her face and hands, and wetting them with his tears.

In his pity for her he understood himself. And when he saw himself as he was, he realized how he had wronged her, how guilty he had been in his pride, in his coldness, even in his anger toward her. He was glad that it was he who was guilty, and that he had nothing to forgive, but that he himself needed forgiveness. She took him to her tiny room, and told him how she lived; but she did not show him the child, nor did she mention the past, knowing how painful it would be to him.

He told her that she must live differently.

"Yes; if I could only live in the country," said she.

"We will talk it over," he said. Suddenly the child began to wail and to scream. She opened her eyes very wide; and, not taking them from her father's face, remained hesitating and motionless.

"Well—I suppose you must feed him," said Michael Ivanovich, and frowned with the obvious effort.

She got up, and suddenly the wild idea seized her to show him whom she loved so deeply the thing she now loved best of all in the world. But first she looked at her father's face. Would he be angry or not? His face revealed no anger, only suffering.

"Yes, go, go," said he; "God bless you. Yes. I'll come again tomorrow, and we will decide. Good-bye, my darling—good-bye." Again he found it hard to swallow the lump in his throat.

When Michael Ivanovich returned to his brother's house, Alexandra Dmitrievna immediately rushed to him.

"Well?"

"Well? Nothing."

"Have you seen?" she asked, guessing from his expression that something had happened.

"Yes," he answered shortly, and began to cry. "I'm getting old and stupid," said he, mastering his emotion.

"No; you are growing wise—very wise."

Three Questions

1. The group of men all gave the King different answers. What might this have told the King?

2. If the King would have known who the wounded man was before he helped him, do you think he would have behaved in the same way? Why?

3. Why didn't the hermit answer the King's question on the first day of his visit?

4. How do you think the King would have responded to the hermit's answers to the questions?

5. What was the difference between the answers the group of men gave and those the hermit gave?

6. Whose answers are most valuable to the King?

7. The King assumed that if he knew the right answers to the three questions, he would never fail. Do you think the answers provided by the hermit would guarantee that the King would never fail?

8. What might this story imply about a person's guarantee of success?

After the Dance

1. This story is written entirely as dialogue. Why might an author choose to do this? Does it have a different effect than if it were told from the perspective of a third-person narrator?

2. How does Varinka's dance with her father affect Ivan? What feelings and thoughts does Ivan have?

3. How does Ivan feel about Varinka's father as he watches them dance?

4. Why do you think Tolstoy chose "The Dance" as the title of the story?

5. Why do you think seeing the man getting beaten has such a powerful effect on Ivan?

6. Do you think Ivan understands good and evil?

7. What effect does Ivan's environment have on how he feels about seeing the beating?

8. Ivan states, "I could not enter the service … and so I have been of no use whatever, as you can see." What does this tell us about a man's role at that time in history? How does it leave Ivan feeling?

9. Why did Tolstoy end the story with the phrase, "And you say … ?"

10. What message might Tolstoy have wanted to convey in this story?

My Dream

Part I

1. Why was Prince Michael so ashamed of his daughter?

2. Tolstoy chose to state some of the dialogue in French. Why do you think he does this, and what effect does it have?

3. In this part of the story, Michael feels great emotional pain. Is he feeling pain for his daughter or for himself?

4. Why does he feel this way?

5. What does this tell us about Michael's character in the early part of the story?

6. With what two conflicting emotions regarding his daughter does Michael struggle?

Part II

1. What do we learn about Lisa's mental state?

2. What did she think of her life as an aristocrat?

3. What changed within Lisa that stopped her from committing suicide?

Part III

1. What do you think finally motivated Michael Ivanovich to go see his daughter?

2. What made Michael feel differently about Lisa?

3. By the end of the story, how did Michael become wiser?

4. To whose dream is Tolstoy referring in the title of the story?

Leo Tolstoy: A Biography
by Cynthia A. Klingel and Robert B. Noyed

T he he most famous works of Leo Tolstoy were two epic novels: **War and Peace** and **Anna Karenina.**

War and Peace is considered one of the greatest novels of all time. It tells of life in Russian society between 1805 and 1815, and it portrays the lives of five aristocratic families. *Anna Karenina,* the shorter of the two novels, is the story of a young woman's passion for a young Russian army officer. In addition to these great books, Tolstoy wrote numerous other stories and accomplished great things during his life.

Tolstoy was born in 1828 at his family's estate, which was south of the city of Moscow in Russia. The family called the estate *Yasnaya Polyana,* which means "Clear Glade" in Russian. Tolstoy would spend most of his life there.

By the time he was nine years old, both of Tolstoy's parents had died, and his aunts then raised him. While living at the family estate in Russia, he was privately educated by French and German tutors. At the age of 16, he enrolled in Kazan

University to study languages and law. He became frustrated with his formal studies and left the university after about three years without earning a degree.

In 1851, Tolstoy and his brother joined the Russian army. It was during his experience as a soldier that he wrote *The Cossacks,* in which he described the life of a young man who had become a cossack, or Russian soldier. After leaving the army, he traveled throughout Europe and visited French and German elementary schools. When he returned to Russia in 1861, he founded a village school at his family's estate, which became known for using teaching methods that were progressive for the time.

Tolstoy married Sonya Andreyevna Bers in 1862. She was a member of a cultured Moscow family, and her father was a physician. Sonya and Leo Tolstoy had 13 children.

All of Tolstoy's original novels and stories were written in Russian and then translated into English and other languages. Along with *War and Peace* and *Anna Karenina,* Tolstoy wrote many stories and novellas that have become popular throughout the world. These include *The Death of Ivan Ilyitch and Other Stories, The Long Exile and Other Stories for Children, God Sees the Truth But Waits, A Prisoner in the Caucasus,* and *The Bear-Hunt.*

As he grew older, Tolstoy often wrote about his views of the reform of Russian society. Tolstoy attacked the inequality and the coercive form of government that existed in Russia. In his essay *What Is Art?* (written in 1898), Tolstoy criticized all classical and modern art, including his own writing, saying that it was done for the cultural elite. He advocated art and writing that was accessible to everyone.

Much has been written about the last days of Tolstoy's life and his death. In 1910, Tolstoy left his wife and family. He arrived at a train station in Astapovo and three days later, on November 7, 1910, he died there. He was 82 years old at the time of his death.

Other Works by Leo Tolstoy

Short Novels

The Cossacks (1863)

The Death of Ivan Ilich (1886)

Master and Man (1989)

The Kreutzer Sonata (1890)

Novels

Childhood (1852)

Boyhood (1854)

Youth (1857)

War and Peace (1865–1869)

Anna Karenina (1875–1877)

Resurrection (1899)

Web Sites about Leo Tolstoy

View pictures of Leo Tolstoy:

http://flag.blackened.net/tolstoy/

Read a biography about Tolstoy:

http://www.kirjasto.sci.fi/ltolstoi.htm

Access 23 of Tolstoy's stories on-line:

http://www.ccel.org/t/tolstoy/23_tales/23_tales.html